BROWNIE & PEARL

Step Out

by CYNTHIA RYLANT
pictures by BRIAN BIGGS

Ready-to-Read

Simon Spotlight
New York London Toronto Sydney New Delhi

Look who is stepping out.
It is Brownie and Pearl!

They are going to a party.

It is a birthday party.

Cats are invited.

There is the house.
See all the balloons?

Now it is time to knock.

Uh-oh.

Brownie feels shy.

Maybe she will go home.

But Pearl is not shy.

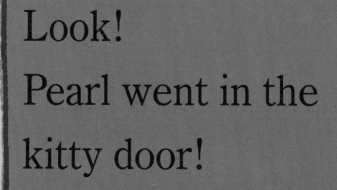

Look!
Pearl went in the
kitty door!

Now Brownie
has to knock.

Welcome to the party, Brownie!

Brownie likes the party.
She plays games.

She eats cake.
She eats ice cream.

She eats more ice cream.

Brownie is happy that
Pearl went in the kitty doo

Pearl is happy too!

BROWNIE & PEARL

Get Dolled Up

by CYNTHIA RYLANT
pictures by BRIAN BIGGS

Ready-to-Read

Simon Spotlight
New York London Toronto Sydney New Delhi

Brownie and Pearl like
to get dolled up.
What shall they wear?

Brownie finds feathers.
Pearl finds pearls.

This is fun!

A little powder?

Yes!

Lipstick?

For Brownie.

Glitter?

See that kitty sparkle!

What about the hair?

Very shiny!

Now some rosy spray.

Time to go out.

"You are so dolled up!"
everyone says.

Brownie and Pearl
know it.

They are feathery.
They are powdery.

They sparkle.
They shine.

They were so
DOLLED UP!

BROWNIE & PEARL
Grab
a Bite

by CYNTHIA RYLANT
pictures by BRIAN BIGGS

Ready-to-Read

Simon Spotlight
New York London Toronto Sydney New Delhi

Time for lunch!
Brownie and Pearl
are going to grab a bite.

What looks good?

Mmm–cheese.

Stringy cheese!

Do not play with your cheese, Pearl.

What else to eat?

Apples. Yum.

Do not roll your apple, Pearl.

Now for something salty.

Saltines, of course.

Brownie likes to bite her saltines into shapes.

Look—P is for Pearl!

Lunch is fun!

Brownie and Pearl need
one more thing:

Milk!

Brownie likes milk
in a glass.
Pearl likes milk in a dish.

Eat, eat.
Drink, drink.

Lick, lick.
Yum.

Lunch!

BROWNIE & PEARL

See the Sights

by CYNTHIA RYLANT
pictures by BRIAN BIGGS

Ready-to-Read

Simon Spotlight
New York London Toronto Sydney New Delhi

Brownie and Pearl are off to see the sights!

Brownie has her handbag.
Pearl has her mouse.
They look very smart.

What to see first?

The hat shop.

Brownie loves hats.

Pearl does too.
What next?

The shoe shop.

Brownie loves shoes.

Pearl does too.

Now what?

The cupcake shop.

Everybody loves cupcakes

Brownie has a big bite.
Pearl has a little bite.

Then Brownie yawns.
Pearl does too.

Cupcakes and sights
have made them sleepy.

Home they go
to nap together.

Sights are good . . .

but home is better.

BROWNIE & PEARL
Go for a Spin

by CYNTHIA RYLANT
pictures by BRIAN BIGGS

Ready-to-Read

Simon Spotlight
New York London Toronto Sydney New Delhi

Look who is coming!
It is Brownie and Pearl.

Brownie has a car.

It has a seat for Pearl.

They are going for a spin.

Brownie drives to
the mailbox.

Pearl gets the mail.

Pearl gets ALL the mail!

Next they deliver the mail.

"Going for a spin?"
someone asks.

YES!
Brownie drives
back home.

She parks her car.
Pearl does not want
to get out.

Pearl will not get out.

Pearl likes the car.

Brownie has an idea.
She runs inside.

Soon she is back.
She has treats.

Pearl is so happy.

She LOVES takeout!

BROWNIE & PEARL

Hit the Hay

by CYNTHIA RYLANT
Pictures by BRIAN BIGGS

Ready-to-Read

Simon Spotlight
New York London Toronto Sydney New Delhi

It is bedtime for
Brownie and Pearl.

First Brownie has
a bath.

Pearl has
a bath too.

Brownie puts on
jammies.

Pearl does not need
jammies.

Time for a snack?

Yes, please!
And a book?

Oh, yes!

Pearl likes the book
about the kitty.

Read it again, please.

Now it is time
to hit the hay.

Brownie and Pearl

go upstairs.

Here is Brownie's room.

Here is Brownie's bed.

It is a cozy bed.

Brownie goes under
the moon covers.

Pearl goes under
the moon covers too.

They curl up.
Happy little bed balls.

Nighty-night, Brownie and Pearl.